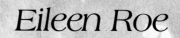

Eileen Roe

Staying with Grandma

illustrated by Jacqueline Rogers

Bradbury Press   New York

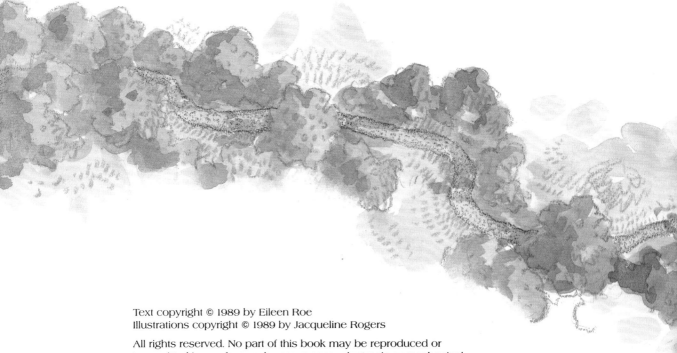

Bradbury Press
An Affiliate of Macmillan, Inc.
866 Third Avenue, New York, NY 10022
Collier Macmillan Canada, Inc.

The text of this book is set in Americana.
Typography by Julie Quan

Printed and bound in Singapore
First American Edition
10 9 8 7 6 5 4 3 2 1

LIBRARY OF CONGRESS CATALOGING-IN-PUBLICATION DATA
Roe, Eileen.
    Staying with Grandma/by Eileen Roe; illustrated by Jacqueline Rogers.
        p.   cm.
    Summary: A child describes a visit to Grandma's house in the country.
    ISBN 0-02-777371-X
    [1. Grandmothers—Fiction.   2. Country life—Fiction.]
I. Rogers, Jackie, ill.   II. Title.
PZ7.R62St   1989
[E]—dc19   87-37611   CIP   AC

For my parents
and grandparents
—E.R.

To Tots and Lucille
—J.R.

When Mommy and Daddy
have someplace to go
and they can't take me along,
I stay at Grandma's house.

Staying with Grandma means
running through the lawn sprinkler
in my bathing suit

and helping Grandma hang sheets
on the line

and having Grandma
push me on the backyard swing

and catching frogs

and picking vegetables
from the garden

and shelling peas
for supper

and taking a walk with Grandma
to watch the sunset

and using a little
of Grandma's bubble bath

and getting my back scratched

and watching the fireflies
dance across the yard

and listening to Grandma
tell a bedtime story.

Staying with Grandma means
having peach jam on toast

and knowing I will come back soon.